DICK WHITTINGTON

Retold by Catherine Storr

Illustrated by Jane Bottomley

Raintree Childrens Books

Milwaukee • Toronto • Melbourne • London

Belitha Press Limited • London

Library of Congress Cataloging in Publication Data

Storr, Catherine.
  Dick Whittington.

  Summary: Retells the traditional tale of the poor boy in
medieval England who made his fortune through his cat
and became Lord Mayor of London.
  1. Whittington, Richard, d. 1423—Juvenile
literature. [1. Whittington, Richard, d. 1423.
2. Folklore—England] I. Title.
PZ8.1.S882Di   1985   398.2'2'09421   85-16904
ISBN 0-8172-2507-2 (lib. bdg.)
ISBN 0-8172-2515-3 (softcover)

Cover printed in the United States;
body printed in Great Britain.
Bound in the United States of America.

1 2 3 4 5 6 7 8 9   90 89 88 87 86

Copyright © in this format Belitha Press Ltd, 1986
Text copyright © Catherine Storr 1986
Illustrations copyright © Jane Bottomley 1986
Art Director: Treld Bicknell

First published in the United States of America 1986
by Raintree Publishers Inc.
330 East Kilbourn Avenue, Milwaukee, Wisconsin 53202
in association with Belitha Press Ltd, London.

Conceived, designed and produced by Belitha Press Ltd,
2 Beresford Terrace, London N5 2DH

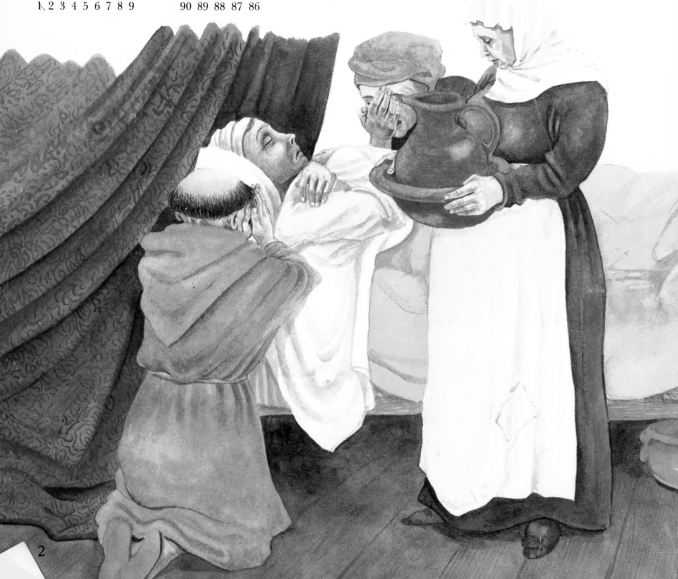

Dick Whittington was the son of a landed
gentleman who lived in the Shire of Glo'ster.
But Dick was only the third son, and when his father
died, he was left very poor. All he had of his own was
a cat. People told him that if he went to London, he
would be able to make his fortune.

At first, Dick did not know how he could get to London. But one day he saw a wagon drawn by eight horses, passing along the high road. It was going to London.

"May I go with you?" Dick asked the wagoner.

"You may. But you will have to walk. There is no room in my wagon for another pair of breeches," the driver said.

So Dick walked beside the wagon and the horses all the long road to London, where he had heard that the streets were paved with gold.

5

At last they reached the Highgate village to the north of the city.

"Here we must say goodbye," the wagoner said. "You walk down that hill, and you will soon be in the city."

Dick stood on Highgate Hill and he looked down at all the houses clustered round tall churches and green parks and along the broad River Thames.

He thought, "There must be so many people down there, all trying to make their fortunes, what chance have I? I might as well go home again. Come on, Cat. Back to the country."

He had picked up his luggage and turned his back on London, when all the church bells of the city below him began to ring. Dick stopped to listen, and it seemed to him that the bells of St. Mary-atte-Bowe were calling to him.

> *Turn again, Whittington,*
> *Thou worthy citizen,*
> *Lord Mayor of London!*

"Lord Mayor! That wouldn't be so bad!" Dick thought, and he turned as the bells told him, and went on his way down the hill into London city.

When he was down among the houses and churches, Dick looked around for the streets of gold. But all he saw were cobbles and mud and dirt and crowds of people, too busy to notice him. He tried to speak to one or two people to ask where he might find somewhere to sleep, something to eat, any work he could do. But everyone was in too much of a hurry to listen.

At last, after several days, Dick was very hungry and very cold and without a home. He found a corner on the steps of a great house in the city, and there he lay down to sleep—or to die.

In the morning he woke, still colder, and still hungrier. At that moment, the door at the top of the steps opened and he saw a woman come out of the house, with her hands full of kitchen scraps. She threw them out to the fowl in the yard.

When she saw Dick, half asleep on the steps below, she began to scold, "What are you doing there, you lazy good-for-nothing? Get away with you, or I shall call the master."

Just then, her master, Mr. Fitzwarren, a rich merchant, appeared at the door. He said, "Hold your noise, woman. Let me hear what this young man has to say for himself."

Then Dick said, "Sir, I am newly come from the country. I had hoped to find work here in the city and to have earned my own bread. But no one stops to listen when I speak."

Mr. Fitzwarren was sorry for the boy. He told the cook to give Dick as much food as he could hold and then to find work for him to do in the kitchens.

"If he is honest and works hard, he shall not be left to die in the street," Mr. Fitzwarren said.

So Dick found a home in the great city of London. He worked hard, and he had food enough. When he first slept in his attic room, he thought he would be kept awake all night by the squeakings and scamperings of the rats and mice who shared the room with him. But it took his cat only a day and a night to get rid of them all.

"What luck," Dick thought, "that my share of my poor father's fortune was my cat! I wonder if I shall be as lucky in time to come?"

He thought that perhaps he might, for his master, Mr. Fitzwarren, was kind to him, and he knew that Miss Alice, Mr. Fitzwarren's daughter, liked him too.

One day, Mr. Fitzwarren called all his servants into his room. He told them that one of his ships was soon going to sail to Africa to trade with the people there. He asked each man and woman whether they wanted to send anything in the ship in the hope of selling it there for a good price. Or if they liked, they could entrust the captain with money to buy goods in Africa which would sell well in England.

Each of the servants had something to send with the ship, except for Dick, who had nothing. Alice offered to lend him money, but this he refused. At last, very sadly, he offered to send his cat, though he could not imagine how she would bring him back any return.

After the merchant ship left London, it sailed for days and weeks till it reached the Barbary Coast of North Africa. There the captain began to trade, selling the goods he had brought from England, and buying spices and silk and jewels to take back again.

The King of the country sent for the captain to show what he had to sell. When the captain arrived at the palace, he found the King and Queen trying to eat a splendid meal. But the tables and floors were covered with rats and mice, who leapt boldly onto the King's own plate and carried off the choicest morsels of food.

The captain was astonished. "Your Majesty, why do you allow these vermin to plague you so?" he asked.

"Alas! We have no way of getting rid of them," the King replied.

"Allow me to send to my ship and I will show you a creature who can help you," the captain said.

Sure enough, no sooner had the cat been brought into the palace, than she leapt on one rat after another, killed a hundred mice, and in no time at all, had cleared every room, so that there was not one of the beasts left.

23

The King was overjoyed. He declared that no matter what the price, he must have the cat for his own. He ordered his servants to bring in chests full of precious stones, jewelry, and gold coins to pay for this rare and precious creature.

The captain, knowing how poor Dick was, and how sad he had been to part with the cat, agreed to sell her for this great treasure. The chests were loaded onto the ship, the King kept the cat, and the captain sailed joyfully back to London.

When the captain returned to Mr. Fitzwarren's house, he told him the story of the cat, and showed him the treasures which the King had sent back for Dick. Mr. Fitzwarren was delighted to hear of the boy's good fortune. He sent a servant to fetch Dick and said, "From now on he is to be called *Mr. Whittington*."

When Dick came in, Mr. Fitzwarren told him that he was now richer than his master. "I will help you, my boy, to make the most of your wealth. We shall soon see you as good a gentleman as any man in the land," he said.

Dick Whittington did indeed become a gentleman and a successful merchant. In time he married Alice Fitzwarren, who had always liked him when he was still a poor working boy. He had his own house, kept a stable of fine horses, and was Lord Mayor of London, as the Bowe Bells had foretold, not once but three times.

He was knighted Sir Richard Whittington, and was rich and grand enough to lend money to the King of England, and to entertain him and his Queen at a magnificent banquet.

And there is still a stone on Highgate Hill to mark the spot where young Dick turned back from his journey to listen to the promise of Bowe Bells.

WHITTINGTON STONE

SIR
RICHARD WHITTINGTON
THRICE LORD MAYOR
OF LONDON
1397 – RICHARD II
1406 – HENRY IV
1420 – HENRY V
SHERIFF – IN 1392

THIS STONE WAS RESTORED
BY J. HILLIER
1935